The Knitting of Elizabeth Amelia

Patricia Lee Gauch

illustrated by

Barbara Lavallee

Henry Holt and Company · New York

Elizabeth Amelia was made of wool. Just where the wool came from no one knew. But her mother found it tucked into a trunk in the attic and took it out and knitted Elizabeth Amelia just the way she wanted her: with apricot-colored arms and sunlit hair and a sky-blue petticoat that she never had to take off.

When she was a baby, it was not a problem that Elizabeth Amelia was made of wool. She bounced better than any of the other babies, and when her mother rocked and cuddled her, she was so soft her mother hummed.

Everyone wanted to hold Elizabeth Amelia.

When she was just a toddler, she rolled around the house, and the cat chose her to sleep with every night. And when she played in the mud on an April day, her mother simply washed her in cool water and hung her up to dry.

She loved the wind.

Of course, she went off to school like all her friends. She walked to school like all her friends and carried her lunch bucket like all her friends. She didn't need a hat: She had one, and she didn't need a coat: She had one.

Everyone loved Elizabeth Amelia at school. They loved to hold her hand when they told stories by the brook and to sit next to her when the wind blew in through the chinks in the one-room schoolhouse.

"Dibs on Elizabeth," they'd say.

No one was as cozy as Elizabeth Amelia.

And that's the way it went
as she grew up. The boys lined up
for her when she got old enough to go to dances,
because she had so much rhythm and so much bounce.

And when they all piled into the convertible, it was Elizabeth
Amelia they put into the middle.

Whatever space they needed to fill, Elizabeth Amelia filled it
just right.

Everyone in town—Mr. Peeples, who never talked; Vance
Morgan, who couldn't stop talking; cranky Grandmother
Singer; even singing Mary Magee—loved Elizabeth Amelia.
She was so warm, so friendly. You could count on Elizabeth
Amelia all the time.

Then one day Elizabeth Amelia got married. James Elmer
was the lucky man. They loved to dance together and take
walks in the woodsy woods. And he loved wool.

It wasn't surprising that Elizabeth Amelia liked to knit. In their little house she knitted wool rugs and lamps, and even wool doors. Before long that house was the coziest, woolliest house in town.

But Elizabeth Amelia had no children. "This won't do," she said one day, scratching her knitted head. "This won't do at all," and she began to search for just the right yarn.

She looked at all the yarn in her basket. There was a warm field brown that was nice. And a sweet sea green— she loved sea green. And a deep cranberry red. "Lovely," said Elizabeth Amelia.

She considered the mint green and sunset orange in a barrel
at the General Store, too. "Good for hats and booties and belts,"
she hummed. She just couldn't decide.

Then one day, she discovered a piece of stray yarn unraveling from her own left foot. It was the color of apricot. "Soft," she said, and she knew it was bouncy. This yarn would do! And borrowing a little wouldn't matter a bit; she was made of wool, after all.

So she began to knit and
knit until she had knitted herself
a sweet baby girl.

How Elizabeth Amelia loved that dear baby! Her name was
True. She was as bouncy as anything, and the cat and the dog
and the lamb from the back field all loved to sleep with her.

Elizabeth Amelia loved True so much, she decided to knit another dear baby. And she did. His name was Bounce. She did have to borrow a little wool from her right foot. But how could that matter? She was made of wool, after all.

"It's nothing, my dear," she said to James Elmer.

"We can still dance!"

The two children brought so much joy to the house, rolling around, laughing, that Elizabeth Amelia just knew they needed a brother and sister. And so she knitted twins: January and February, she called them, after her favorite months. She knitted a little yarn from her right leg and purled a little from her left. There was nothing like soft and springy wool to make a dear baby!

Now four kids bounced around and cuddled by the fire. They told stories, kept their mother and father laughing all the time, and filled the clothesline on washing day.

Of course, Elizabeth Amelia—wool or not—didn't get around as much as she used to—and one day for a split second, she worried about that, but only for a second. She could still rock as much as she wanted. And laughing and rocking were what she liked to do best.

And so when the kids needed new shoes or new mittens, she didn't even go to the store. She just unraveled a little bit more from herself—an elbow, or a shoulder—and knitted what they needed right on the spot.

The trouble was, one day when James Elmer came into the room, he just stared at her. "Elizabeth Amelia," he said. "You're nothing but a pillow!"

Elizabeth Amelia looked. Why, indeed, she had knitted almost all of herself away.

The next morning James almost sat on her by mistake.
"Elizabeth," he shouted. "This won't do! We haven't danced for
months. We can't go for walks. The children need a mother!"
But what could a pillow say!

Bounce didn't wait for the pillow to say anything. He didn't know anything about knitting, and there was no yarn in the basket. But he remembered kitchen curtains knitted the color of lemon and ran to get them. January and February always liked the blue of their bedside lamp and ran to get that. James Elmer pulled the crimson cloth right off the dining room table.

But it was True who bounded up the attic
stairs. Could there be yarn in Grandmother's trunk?
She searched and, yes, there was—it was the color of
apricot, and bouncy!

When True climbed down with the yarn,
Elizabeth Amelia whispered, "Yes!" and she picked
up the needles and started to knit. It wasn't perfect—pillows
aren't the best knitters—but Elizabeth Amelia never once said,
"Oops, I've lost a stitch," and no one else said, "You've purled a
whole row, Elizabeth Amelia, you were supposed to knit."

Now Elizabeth Amelia grew right
before their eyes. She grew legs and
hips, a chest and neck and ears. She
liked the new colors so much, she
knitted a new hairdo for herself
and a new dress and finally
new shoes: they were crimson
because she was hoping she
and James Elmer might go
dancing again.

It had been a long time.

"You're beautiful, Elizabeth Amelia," James Elmer said when she was finished.

"Well, I am, aren't I?" said Elizabeth Amelia.

Everyone was glad that she was back—all of her—and everyone came over to sit next to her by the fire and to admire her new hairdo, her new dress, and her new crimson shoes.

When she was home, that is, because . . .

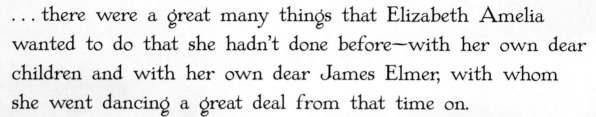

. . . there were a great many things that Elizabeth Amelia
wanted to do that she hadn't done before—with her own dear
children and with her own dear James Elmer, with whom
she went dancing a great deal from that time on.